**Put Beginning Readers on the Right Track with
ALL ABOARD READING™**

The All Aboard Reading series is especially for beginning readers. Written by noted authors and illustrated in full color, these are books that children really and truly *want* to read—books to excite their imagination, tickle their funny bone, expand their interests, and support their feelings. With three different reading levels, All Aboard Reading lets you choose which books are most appropriate for your children and their growing abilities.

Level 1—for Preschool through First Grade Children
Level 1 books have very few lines per page, very large type, easy words, lots of repetition, and pictures with visual "cues" to help children figure out the words on the page.

Level 2—for First Grade to Third Grade Children
Level 2 books are printed in slightly smaller type than Level 1 books. The stories are more complex, but there is still lots of repetition in the text and many pictures. The sentences are quite simple and are broken up into short lines to make reading easier.

Level 3—for Second Grade through Third Grade Children
Level 3 books have considerably longer texts, use harder words and more complicated sentences.

All Aboard for happy reading!

Lucinda McQueen, because you drew
Delightful pictures, and still do,
And shared with us what you knew,
We dedicate this book to you!

Library of Congress Cataloging-in-Publication Data

Buller, Jon, 1943–
    The video kids / by Jon Buller and Susan Schade.
      p.   cm. — (All aboard reading)
    Summary: The Machine that Jerome and Curtis have made in the garage causes them to be
sucked into their new video game, where they try to perform impossible tasks while avoiding
the Four Evil Frogs.
    [1. Video games—Fiction. 2. Inventions—Fiction. 3. Science fiction.] I. Schade,
Susan. II. Title. III. Series.
PZ7. B9135Vi 1994
[E]—dc20   93-26923
                                                                  CIP
ISBN 0-448-40181-9 (GB)   A B C D E F G H I J   AC

ISBN 0-448-40180-0 (pbk.) A B C D E F G H I J

ALL
ABOARD
READING™

Level 3
Grades 2-3

THE VIDEO KIDS

By Jon Buller
and Susan Schade

Grosset & Dunlap • New York

My real name is Jerome. But I am better known as the Video Kid. My friend Curtis started calling me that when I got to Level 30 of "Super Disaster Master."

Curtis is a Video Kid, too. But he's not as good as I am. He's only up to Level 11.

Curtis and I have a secret club.

We meet and play in Curtis's garage.

There is paper taped over the windows so nobody can steal our video game secrets.

Or spy on THE MACHINE!

The Machine is our invention. It takes up almost the whole garage.

Curtis started building it before I even knew him. In fact, I happen to know that the very first parts of the Machine were Curtis's old stroller and a windup teddy bear music box.

Now we use broken VCRs, old TV

sets, computer parts, vacuum cleaners…
whatever we can get. The Machine has
two different sections. We call them Pods.

Curtis knows all about machines. He
reads *Mad Scientist Magazine* every week.
But even Curtis was surprised when we
discovered the awesome power of the
Machine!

I had brought over my newest game. It was called "The Sultan's Ten Impossible Tasks." I was hoping that together we could figure out how to destroy the Four Evil Frogs without getting eaten alive. So far they had gotten me every time.

I told Curtis how "The Sultan's Ten Impossible Tasks" has ten levels. If you do all ten, you get to marry the sultan's beautiful daughter and live in the Palace of the Moon. But if you fail at any one task, you DIE!

"See the hourglass in the corner?" I said. "That shows how much time you have left. When you do something good, like get a weapon, you get more sand. When you do something stupid, like crash into a Radish-head, the sand runs out faster."

I was explaining all of this to Curtis when I felt somebody breathing on the back of my neck.

"SPIES!"

We both whipped around.

It was only Curtis's little sister.

"Ew, it's Lump," Curtis said. He calls her Lump when their parents aren't around. He says it's because he remembers the good old days when she was nothing but a lump in their mother's belly. She hates it.

"What do you think you're doing in here?" asked Curtis.

"Nothing," she said. "And don't call me Lump! Can I play, too?"

"No. You can get out. You're too little," Curtis told her. "We're splitting fractals and you might get hurt."

Lump stuck her tongue out at Curtis, and ran out before he could get her back.

"What's a fractal? And how do you split one?" I asked Curtis.

He shrugged his shoulders. "Beats me," he said. "It's on the cover of the latest *Mad Scientist Magazine*. I haven't read it yet."

We decided to work on Pod Two of the Machine for a while.

You can get right inside Pod Two. Curtis went in, and I followed him. I put my Sultan game on the dashboard.

We aren't sure what happened next.
Curtis says I bumped the game with my
elbow and knocked it into the slot. I say
the Machine slurped it up.

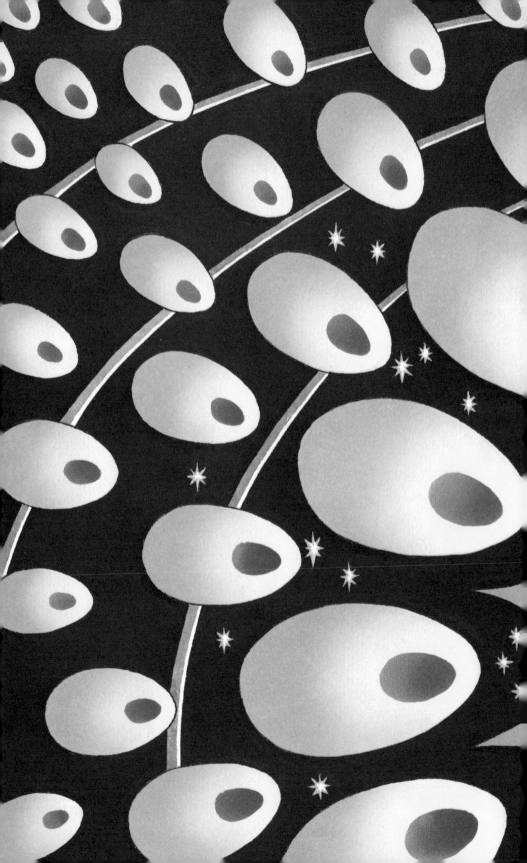

There was a loud WHOOSH, a zillion colored lights, and then everything went black.

When the lights came on again, Curtis and I stumbled to our feet and looked around.

The ground was bright orange, and the sky was green. We were standing in a city of gleaming domes and towers. I recognized it right away.

"Holy cow!" I shouted. "We're <u>inside</u> my video game!"

"Hmmm," said Curtis. "The Machine is even more powerful than I thought."

We laughed and gave each other a high five.

"Hey! Look at this!" Curtis said,
jumping up in the air about twenty feet.
"Cool!"

We were bouncing around and yucking
it up when the sultan appeared in the sky.

"It is time to begin the first impossible task," he boomed, "<u>if</u> you value your lives!" He gave an evil chuckle and faded away.

<u>Oodle deedle um tee dum.</u> The ground started moving.

I fell down. It hurt. And there was blood on my elbow.

That's when I started to worry. Maybe this was no game! Maybe it was for real! I thought about the Four Evil Frogs. If only we had fallen into "Super Disaster Master" instead!

We had to run to keep from falling down.

"Hey cool! Here's a tunnel!" Curtis shouted as he disappeared into a black doorway.

I was right behind him. Just before I went in, I looked up. The hourglass had appeared in the sky. And the grains of sand were slipping down already.

If this was real, what was going to happen to us when the last grain of sand dropped down?

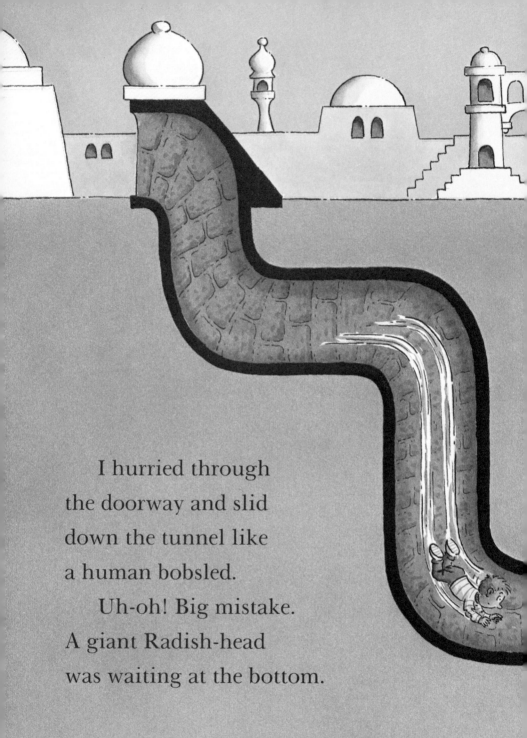

I hurried through
the doorway and slid
down the tunnel like
a human bobsled.

Uh-oh! Big mistake.
A giant Radish-head
was waiting at the bottom.

"Eeahhh!" Curtis almost fainted.

"Jump on the spring!" I shouted.

We went so high, we shot up into
outer space.

A flying carpet whooshed by. Curtis
and I hopped on. "Now we can get some
star weapons," I told him. We desperately
needed weapons.

BWAM! BWAM! We crashed into some stars. One exploded into a silver net. Another exploded into a light sword. Now we had weapons and lots more sand in the hourglass.

Curtis loved it! He was standing up and waving the light sword around like a pirate.

"Be careful!" I cried.

A flaming asteroid was streaking across the sky toward us. It kept coming and coming.

KA-BOOM! It smashed into us.

We lost the magic carpet. The sand started running out faster. And we were falling. Falling through space.

We landed on a narrow ledge.

There were bottomless black pits on either side of us. And I knew what was waiting for us at the end of the ledge. The Four Evil Frogs!

"Hey, look, Jerome! My sword got bigger!" Curtis was excited.

The net seemed bigger, too, and heavier. This was serious.

"It didn't get bigger," I said grimly. "We got smaller!" I didn't tell him, but I could see right through him, too!

SPROING! Another Radish-head sprouted in our path!

Curtis yelled, "Prepare to fry, Vegetable Breath!" Then he zapped the Radish-head with his light sword.

But instead of disappearing, it split into four Radish-heads! It was the light sword that disappeared.

"Oh, no! This is it!" I thought. "This is the end."

I threw my silver net at them. I didn't know what else to do. And suddenly I had a net full of Radish-heads.

Curtis was looking ahead while I struggled with the net.

"YIPES! There they are!" Curtis yelled.

I looked up, and fear made me weak.

The Four Evil Frogs were waiting for us in the distance. They were grinning.

I gulped. Now it really was all over. We had no weapons. We were little and see-through. All we had was a net full of Radish-heads.

There was no way those Frogs weren't going to eat us.

That's when I had an idea.

"Curtis!" I cried. "I bet we can feed the Radish-heads to the Frogs! Then we only have nine more Impossible Tasks until we marry the beautiful princess!"

"Marry!" Curtis shrieked. "Marry!!?"

I glanced at the hourglass. Not much sand left.

"I'm too young!" he cried. "I don't want to get married! Do you?"

"No," I said. "Of course not. But that's the game. Come on. Time's running out!"

"Oh no," said Curtis. "Nobody's tricking me into marriage. Not even a beautiful princess!" And he started turning around.

"Wait!" I yelled. "There's no turning back!"

6

But Curtis was already turning around.

The ledge crumbled beneath his feet. He fell!

I dropped the Radish-heads, threw myself on the ground, and grabbed his foot.

Curtis was dangling there, over the bottomless pit. The sand was almost gone. The Four Evil Frogs were hopping toward us. And I couldn't hold on much longer. We were in serious trouble.

Then I saw relief spread over Curtis's upside-down face.

I looked up.

Above us was a video screen filled with a huge head. It was Curtis's little sister! What was going on? Then it hit me. She was watching us from the other side of the Machine.

"LUMP!" Curtis yelled. "Save us!"

She said something. I couldn't hear her, but I could see her lips moving.

"There's no hope, Curtis," I cried. "She's only a little kid. She doesn't know how to play."

"Yes, she does," Curtis said. "Push the reset button, Lump! It's on the left."

She looked madder. It looked like she was saying, "Don't call me Lump!"

"Okay, okay!" Curtis said. "Please save us, Lavinia!"

The next thing I knew, we were lying
on the floor of the garage, panting. We
were our regular size and you couldn't
see through us anymore.

Curtis was muttering, "Saved...saved."
And Lavinia was saying, "<u>Now</u> can I
play?"

That was a few weeks ago.

We decided to let Lavinia be in the club since she saved our lives. Besides, we needed to swear her to secrecy.

We are making some minor adjustments to the Machine, and Lavinia is dying to try it out.

That should be interesting.